# Dear Parents:

Congratulations! Your child is taking the first steps on an exciting journey. The destination? Independent reading!

**STEP INTO READING®** will help your child get there. The program offers five steps to reading success. Each step includes fun stories and colorful art or photographs. In addition to original fiction and books with favorite characters, there are Step into Reading Non-Fiction Readers, Phonics Readers and Boxed Sets, Sticker Readers, and Comic Readers—a complete literacy program with something to interest every child.

## Learning to Read, Step by Step!

### Ready to Read    Preschool–Kindergarten
• big type and easy words • rhyme and rhythm • picture clues
For children who know the alphabet and are eager to begin reading.

### Reading with Help    Preschool–Grade 1
• basic vocabulary • short sentences • simple stories
For children who recognize familiar words and sound out new words with help.

### Reading on Your Own    Grades 1–3
• engaging characters • easy-to-follow plots • popular topics
For children who are ready to read on their own.

### Reading Paragraphs    Grades 2–3
• challenging vocabulary • short paragraphs • exciting stories
For newly independent readers who read simple sentences with confidence.

### Ready for Chapters    Grades 2–4
• chapters • longer paragraphs • full-color art
For children who want to take the plunge into chapter books but still like colorful pictures.

**STEP INTO READING®** is designed to give every child a successful reading experience. The grade levels are only guides; children will progress through the steps at their own speed, developing confidence in their reading.

Remember, a lifetime love of reading starts with a single step!

# AWESOME TALES!

Manufactured under license granted to AMEET Sp. z o.o.
by the LEGO Group.

AMEET Sp. z o.o.
Nowe Sady 6, 94–102 Łódź—Poland
ameet@ameet.eu
www.ameet.eu

www.LEGO.com

Published in the United States by Random House Children's Books, a division of Penguin Random House
LLC, 1745 Broadway, New York, NY 10019, and in Canada by Penguin Random House Canada Limited,
Toronto.

Step into Reading, Random House, and the Random House colophon are registered trademarks of
Penguin Random House LLC.

Visit us on the Web!
rhcbooks.com

Educators and librarians, for a variety of teaching tools, visit us at RHTeachersLibrarians.com

ISBN 978-0-593-43154-2 (trade)

MANUFACTURED IN CHINA

10 9 8 7 6 5 4 3 2 1

Random House Children's Books supports the First Amendment and celebrates the right to read.

# AWESOME TALES!

A Collection of Five Early Readers

Random House 🏠 New York

# CONTENTS

# LEGO CITY

# Birthday Helpers!

by Steve Foxe

based on the story by Stacia Deutsch

illustrated by AMEET Studio

Random House 🏠 New York

Harl Hubbs jumped out of bed.
"It is my birthday!" he shouted.
Harl loved helping
the people in the city.
To celebrate his birthday,
Harl wanted to help
as many people
as he possibly could.

He rushed outside
to get started!

The first person Harl ran into was Lieutenant Duke DeTain. Duke was a police officer who knew a thing or two about flips and jump-kicks. "Hello, Helpful Handyman!" Duke said.

"Today is my birthday,"
said Harl.
He was planning to have
a happy, helpy day.
Harl picked up his toolbox.
"Need anything?" he asked Duke.

"No, it is a quiet day in the city,"
said Duke.
"Let me know if there is
anything exciting to do."

The next person Harl saw
was Firefighter Bob.
"Need any help?" Harl asked.
"Nope," Bob replied with a yawn.

But Harl had an idea—
and a screwdriver!

Before Bob could stop him,
Harl fixed the siren
on the fire truck
to sound louder than ever.

BOCK! BOCK! BOCK!

Bob pressed the siren button.

*Bock! Bock! Bock!*

The siren sounded like a chicken!

Before Harl could fix it,

a fire alarm went off.

Firefighter Bob raced
to an emergency.
Harl felt bad that his help
had not gone as planned.

Down the street, Harl saw Poppy Starr.

Her stage was in pieces!

Harl got out his hammer to help.

When Poppy turned around,

the stage was fully built.

"Ta-da!" Harl said with pride.

"Thanks, Harl," Poppy replied.

"But I was taking the stage down,

not putting it up!"

Then Harl saw Shirley Keeper
carrying an empty trash can.
"I am having a rough day,"
Harl told her.
"Me too," Shirley said.
"Not much trash to collect today."

Harl whipped out his toolbox.

"I could upgrade your truck!"

he offered.

"No thanks," Shirley replied.

"But maybe you can join me
on my route tomorrow."
Harl frowned.
Tomorrow would not be
his special day anymore.

Duke DeTain walked by.
"Nothing exciting
is happening today,"
Harl told Duke with a big sigh.

"It is the worst birthday ever."

"But the day is not over yet!"

Duke said.

Harl headed home.

He was sad that he had not helped anyone.

Then someone knocked on his door.

It was Chief McCloud.

She asked Harl to help her

untangle some lights.

Next, Mayor Fleck stopped by.

"Can you pick up my groceries?"

Harl was happy to help!

Harl fixed the lights and then picked up the mayor's groceries. On his way to deliver the food, he ran into Police Chief Wheeler.

He needed Harl
to fix
the front wheel
on his skateboard.

Harl was happy to help.
Chief Wheeler gave Harl
his skateboard, and he carried
the mayor's groceries for Harl.

Harl followed Chief Wheeler

back to the police station

to get the chief's spare wheels.

When he opened the door,

he saw that all his friends were there!

"Happy birthday, Harl!"

everyone shouted.

The lights that Harl had untangled

had been strung up for the party.

And the groceries he had picked up

included a big birthday cake!

Firefighter Bob thanked Harl
for fixing the siren on the truck.
The clucking sounds had helped him
rescue some lost baby chicks.

Poppy Starr was grateful, too.
Her record company wanted
to hold a last-minute concert tonight,
and now her stage was all set!
Even Shirley was excited—
she would have so much trash
to pick up after Harl's party!

Duke thanked Harl for helping
so many people.

Harl was glad, but he realized he had
never found anything exciting
for Duke to do.

"Fighting crime is great,"
Duke said with a grin.

"But planning your
top-secret surprise party
was super exciting!"

Harl was so happy.

It turned out that he had

helped his friends all day long!

It was a happy, helpy day.

"This is the best birthday ever!"

Harl shouted.

## Costume Capers

by Steve Foxe

based on the story by Kelly McKain

illustrated by AMEET Studio

Random House 🏠 New York

Mayor Fleck's alarm clock blared.

"Good thing I got a full night's

rest," he said.

"I have so much work to do

before the big Halloween party."

Mayor Fleck jumped out of bed

to start his very busy day.

But something felt . . . wrong.

"My corn outfit!" he cried.

"I never take it off!"

It was gone.

Mayor Fleck put on
the only other suit he owned
and rushed to Town Hall.
Planning the Halloween party
couldn't wait.

But his assistant, Carol,

stopped him at the door.

"Excuse me, sir," she said.

"The mayor is not in yet."

"I am the mayor!"

he shouted.

"Do you not recognize me?"

Carol squinted at the mayor.
Without his corn suit,
she really did not recognize him!
Neither did Carol's daughter,
Madison.

"Mommy, who is this
strange man?" she asked.
Carol frowned and looked
closer and closer, until . . .
She gasped. "ARGH! It *is* you!
But, sir, you do not *look* like you!"

Carol was not the only one
who had trouble recognizing
Mayor Fleck.

At the new construction site,
no one would work until
the "real" mayor showed up
to sign off on the permits.

"Nice costume, buddy,"
the foreman joked.
"It will be a real hit
at the Halloween party."

It only got worse

as the day went on.

At the new shopping center,

they would not let Mayor Fleck

cut the ceremonial ribbon,

so they could not start working!

And at the opening

of the hospital's new wing,

the doctors thought

Mayor Fleck was just

a confused patient

who had bonked his head.

Carol was getting worried.

"If no one believes

you are the mayor,

you cannot plan the party!"

Then Madison had an idea.
"It is almost Halloween—
you just need a costume!
That way everyone will
recognize you."

Mayor Fleck put on

the airplane outfit

Madison had found for him.

"What does this button do?"

he asked with a smile.

Uh-oh!

The propeller started to spin,
and the mayor flew up in the air!
*WHOOSH!*

"Heeeeelp!" he cried
as he shot across the room
and right out the window.

Mayor Fleck crash-landed
on Harl the Handyman's bicycle!
"Thanks for breaking my fall,"
the mayor said as he took off
the airplane costume.

"Happy to help, flying stranger,"
Harl replied.

He did not recognize the mayor!

Mayor Fleck explained the situation,
and Harl had the perfect solution.

"You can borrow my tutu!" he said.

At his office, Mayor Fleck realized
the tutu was not right.
And to make matters worse,
his pen suddenly turned
into a banana!

He started to panic.

How could he get his work done

for the Halloween party

if no one believed

he was the mayor?

Just then, Fire Chief Freya McCloud
climbed through his office window.
"Try this on for size," she said,
handing Mayor Fleck
a ninja costume and a set of nunchucks.

But the nunchucks slipped right out
of his hands and flew across the room.
"All this smashing is distracting!" he cried.
"This outfit is not helpful for my work."

"Have no fear—Duke DeTain is here!"

the top cop shouted,

entering through the window

and rolling over the mayor's desk.

"We will find Mayor Fleck

a more colorful costume

to wear to the party!"

Mayor Fleck felt that something
very strange
was going on.
Where had Duke
come from?
And how had his pen
turned into a banana?

Before Mayor Fleck could
figure out what was happening,
Madison and her friends arrived
with more costumes.

His brain started to boggle.

"Stop this! No more!" he shouted.

No one listened.

There was a whole

avalanche of costumes!

"Help!" wailed the mayor.

"This is scarier than any

Halloween movie marathon!

It is a nightmare!"

# BEEP! BEEP! BEEP!

The mayor recognized that sound.

It was his alarm clock!

He gasped.

"It really *had* been a nightmare,"

he said.

"I would never wear

such silly costumes in real life.

And no wonder those weird

things were happening!"

Best of all, Mayor Fleck's
corn suit was right where
he had left it: on his body.
"This is the perfect costume
for the Halloween party . . . and
for every other day of the year!"

# The Perfect Trick

by Steve Foxe

based on the story by Matt Killeen

illustrated by AMEET Studio

Random House New York

It was a typical day at
police headquarters.
That meant another case was
closed by Sergeant Sam Grizzled
and Detective Rooky Partnur!
"Your days as a thief are over,"
Rooky told their latest criminal.
"I do not know why
you are so excited, Rooky,"
Sam grumbled.
"It is just police work."

Rooky smiled and opened an envelope
she found on her desk.

"Wow!" she shouted.

"Looks like I won tickets
to the stunt show!"

"Come with me to watch it?"

she asked Sam. "You will love it."

Sam was not so sure, but he

agreed to go with his partner.

A huge crowd showed up
on the night of the stunt show.
Everyone was bouncing
up and down in their seats,
Rooky included.

All of a sudden, the stadium went dark—
except for one pool of light.
"Now I cannot see my hot dog,"
Sam complained.

A motorcycle rider burst into the arena.

"That is Rocket Racer!"

Rooky yelled. "My favorite!"

Rocket Racer waved to the audience
and sped toward a ramp.

The barrels near it caught fire.

The stadium screamed in excitement!

The mind-blowing stunts went on.

Monster trucks leapt over cars.

There were explosions and giant robots.

Rooky jumped up and down.

Her mouth hung open in awe.

"This is . . . awesome," Rooky said.

Sam was having trouble staying awake.

"What use are stunts in the real world?"

he asked.

Rooky did not hear him. She was busy
thinking back to when she was a kid,
doing tricks on her skateboard!

The next day,

Rooky brought her skateboard

to the police station.

"I found it!" she shouted,

waving the dusty skateboard around.

"I do not know why I ever stopped

riding it."

Every day on their lunch break,

Rooky and Sam went to the skate park.

Rooky practiced a lot,

but the tricks were really hard.

While Sam ate doughnuts and napped,

Rooky went up the ramp, into the air . . .

and onto the ground.

Suddenly, a voice said,

"You know what the problem is?"

It was Rocket Racer!

Rocky gasped.

"What are you doing here?" she asked.

"I need to practice, too," Rocket explained.

Rocket sat Rooky down.

"Practice the push, stop, and turn,"
Rocket said.

"Learn one trick at a time.
Work smarter, not harder."

With Rocket's help, Rooky chose one trick
and put all her effort into it.
After she got it right, she did it again
and again, until it was perfect!

Suddenly, Sam and Rooky's radios

burst to life.

"All units. Hacksaw Hank

has robbed the doughnut shop . . . ,"

said the dispatcher.

"That is next door!" Rooky cried.

Just then, Hacksaw Hank leapt over
the park wall with a huge bag of cash.
He spotted Sam and Rooky
and ran for the gate.

"Stop, in the name of the law!"

shouted Rooky.

One of the other skateboarders

jumped into Hacksaw's path.

The crook lost his grip.

He dropped the cash onto

the boy's lap and ran off.

Springing into action, Rooky chased
the robber on her board.
The crook had a head start,
but she could still catch up. . . .

Hank darted into the street
with Rooky hot on his heels.
He wove through a traffic jam.

Push! Turn!

Rooky handled the board

like a pro, catching up fast.

Then a helicopter roared overhead.

Clara the Criminal leaned out and dropped

a rope ladder down to the street!

Rooky had to get in front of Hank

or he would escape!

Rooky leaned right,

toward a wooden ramp.

With a jump, she hit the ramp

and soared into the air.

Rooky gripped the side

of her board and sailed

over Hank's head.

She landed in front of him
and handcuffed his wrists.
It was the perfect trick!
"I would clap, but I cannot
move my hands," said Hank.

Back at the skate park,
Rooky thanked all her new
skateboarding friends for their help—
especially Rocket Racer!

Sam looked sheepish.

"I was . . . wrong," he mumbled.

"Doing something you love
makes you a better person . . .
and a better cop."

"Gee, thanks, Grizzled!"

Rooky smiled, blushing.

"Hey, I have eight minutes

of lunch left.

Think I can nail the kickflip?"

# A Wild Life

by Steve Foxe

based on the story by Joshua Pruett

illustrated by AMEET Studio

Random House 🏠 New York

A TV host was speaking
into a camera.
"I am Westbrook W. Sleet,
and this is *Wild Wilderness*!
Today we are in the jungle filming
an animal rescue camp,"
Westbrook said.

"Uhh, look behind you,"
said Toby, the cameraman,
when he spotted a lioness
crouched behind Westbrook.
"Should we run?"

"YES!" Westbrook yelled.

"But keep the camera rolling!"

The two men ran into the animal

rescue camp. So did the lioness.

Inside the camp, a woman calmly
tossed a chunk of meat to the
lioness and petted its head.
"Mina was not chasing you,"
the woman explained.
"She has a sore paw
and just wanted a snack."

"I am Lydia Lighthouse,

chief veterinarian," the woman said.

"Let me give you a tour."

Lydia's team looked after many

wild animals, including Mina

and other lion friends.

Also on staff were
veterinarian Mikko, pilot Carla,
and driver Perry.
The camp had all kinds
of special equipment
and vehicles.

"Here is a great shot, Toby,"

Westbrook said,

standing near an elephant.

Toby started filming just as

the elephant showered Westbrook

with water from its trunk!

Toby tried not to laugh.

Next, Westbrook spotted a crocodile,
but Toby realized it was actually
a toy for the monkeys.

*"Ooh, ooh!"* shouted a monkey.

She hugged Westbrook.

"Meet Ivy," said Lydia.

"We found her injured as an infant
and nursed her back to health.
This little prankster has grown up
in the camp."

Suddenly, Ivy stole
the microphone!

Westbrook tried to get it back.

Meanwhile, Toby was very bored.

He filmed a pile of banana peels.

"This footage is not exciting,"

Westbrook said, disappointed.

Just then, an alarm sounded.

It was an animal emergency!

Lydia and her crew

jumped into action.

There was not a second to lose!

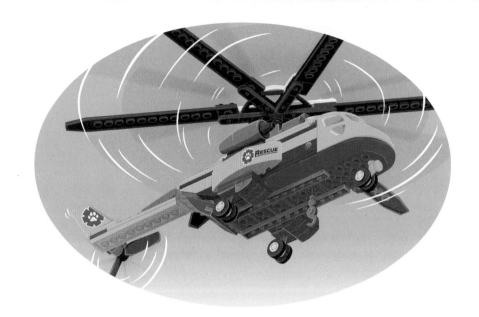

"To the river!" Lydia shouted.

Carla led the way in her helicopter.

Westbrook felt like he was in a movie.

At the riverbed,

the team heard the cry

of a baby animal.

But where was it?

"The sound is coming from

this direction," said Perry,

pointing to the shoreline.

Westbrook and Toby offered to help.

Lydia gave them a flying drone.

"We need a bird's-eye view,"

she said.

"Perfect. I always wanted
to be a bird," joked Westbrook.
Toby stopped filming and launched
the drone into the air.
A small screen showed them
what the drone's camera saw.

"I see it!" Westbrook cried.

"It is a lion cub trapped
between the rocks."

Then he noticed something else
on the screen.

"Wait! There is that
inflatable crocodile again."

Lydia looked at the screen.

"That is a real croc!" she said.

"We need to rescue

the lion cub right now!"

The team worked together to
clear a path for the cub while Toby
and Lydia distracted the
crocodile with some meat snacks.

Toby had never seen a real
crocodile so close before, but he
tried to be as brave as he could.

Then it was Westbrook's turn.

It was all up to him.

He leaned into the riverbed

and reached out to the cub.

"You can trust me,"

Westbrook said calmly.

The animal was scared at first,

but it eventually jumped

into Westbrook's arms.

Everyone cheered!

The lion cub was saved.

On the ride back to the camp,
Westbrook held the sleeping
cub on his lap.
"I am happy that we helped,
but I am afraid our TV show
is now an endangered species,"
he said sadly.

"I tried to film the rescue," Toby said.

"But my camera disappeared.

All I found was this banana peel."

Lydia burst out laughing.
"Ivy must have taken it!"
she said.

The team returned to camp.
Ivy was waiting for them.
She had the camera!

Toby traded Ivy a banana

for the camera.

To his surprise, the clever monkey

had recorded the entire rescue!

Everyone was thrilled!

The show would go on.

Toby set up the camera for one
last shot. Ivy peeked through
the camera lens.

"Friendship is the
greatest adventure!"
Westbrook exclaimed.
Suddenly, there was a *ROAR*.
It was Mina the lioness!
She was staring at Toby's camera
and did not seem happy.

Mina chased Toby
and Westbrook back into
the jungle.
"Keep it rolling, Ivy,"
cried Westbrook.
"This is the exciting part!"

# The Fire Spirit

by Steve Foxe

based on a story from the Fire Department archives
by Maciej Andrysiak

illustrated by AMEET Studio

Random House 🏠 New York

All the firefighters at
the fire station
were watching the news closely.
A space shuttle was supposed
to land that day, but it was gone
from the radar!

"I have a tale
    to lighten the mood,"
    said Fire Chief Chandler.
"It is about . . .
    the legendary Fire Spirit!"

"I saw it in the woods once,

surrounded by smoke,"

Chief Chandler said.

"The ground where it had walked

was scorched to ash!"

Some of the older firefighters

smiled and laughed,

but Horace and Bart hung on

to every word the chief said.

Just then, the door flew open.

It was Sam Eaglet,

the station's trusty pilot.

The fire chief smiled at her.

Horace dreamed of flying
a plane like Sam's.
In fact, he was staring at Sam's
pilot helmet long enough
for Sam to notice.
"You will make it to the skies
someday, kid," she said.
"But try practicing with
your fire extinguisher first."

Horace did not have long
to think about Sam's words,
because just then,
the alarm sounded!
"Prepare the fire engines!"
Fire Chief Chandler shouted.
It was time to slide down
the fire pole!

Horace needed

to suit up.

Horace noticed that Bart
was munching on something.
"Where did you get that meatball?"
he asked. "From the kitchen!"
Bart replied.
"I, uhh . . . borrowed it
from the chef."

Once the firefighters
had made it into the woods,
Fire Chief Chandler tossed
Horace an extinguisher.
"Let's get these flames put out!"
The fire chief said.

As Horace and Bart worked,
Sam's plane flew overhead,
ready to release water.
"'Practice with my fire
extinguisher,' huh?"
Horace said to himself.

Horace mounted the
extinguisher like a horse
and released the valve.
The fire extinguisher shot
into the air with Horace aboard!

As the brave firefighter flew,
the foam splashed the trees,
putting out the flames.
But then the extinguisher
started to run out of foam!

Horace steered around the trees,

but he eventually hit a branch

and landed face-first in the dirt.

"I guess I need to practice

landing, too," Horace

said to himself.

While he brushed his knees off,

he noticed a strange figure

standing in front of him,

surrounded by smoke.

"Help! Help!" Horace cried.

"The Fire Spirit!"

The strange figure
reached out a hand
and touched Horace
on the shoulder.
"Are you all right?"
Horace heard the figure say.
"Do not eat me!" Horace shouted,
backing away.

Just then, he heard

a whooshing noise behind

the Fire Spirit.

It was Bart, riding his own

extinguisher like a rocket!

"Leave my friend alone!"

Bart yelled.

The Fire Spirit ducked,

and Bart flew straight

into a tree trunk.

As the smoke cleared,

Horace and Bart could see

the Fire Spirit more clearly.

They watched as it

took off its helmet.

"And I thought nothing
could surprise me
after traveling to space,"
the figure said.

Horace jumped for joy.

"You are not the Fire Spirit,"

he said.

"You are an astronaut from that

lost shuttle!"

"The shuttle did not get lost,"

the astronaut replied.

"It had a fuel leak

and I had to make

an emergency landing.

But then the fuel caught on fire!"

"Well, the fire is all clear now,"
Fire Chief Chandler said.
He and the other firefighters
gathered around to
welcome the astronaut.
But Bart was not there.
Horace looked up to find his friend
still in the tree branches.
"I will be down after
I finish this snack!" Bart said.

Back at the station,

Horace watched the astronaut

give interviews on TV.

All was safe and calm again . . .

until Sam burst through the door!

Sam tossed her pilot cap
in front of Horace.
"Anyone who can fly
a fire extinguisher like that
deserves a chance to
fly a real plane," Sam said.

Horace put on the cap happily.

"Lessons start tomorrow,"

Sam said.

"I can see you have

the Fire Pilot Spirit!"